You are one in a Chameleon

By Monica Robinson

To Scott for being my love bird.

To all the other special people in my life who have shown me love.

John 4:16

I can't stop RAVEN about us.

Ravens are crafty birds; they can undo velcro fasteners and unzip zippers to steal food.

You won me over from the GECKO

A gecko can walk on walls
because of the billions of
tiny, sticky filaments on its
toe pads.

There's no way to CAMELflage the way I feel about you because...

Camels move both legs on one side of the body at the same time.

...there are too many things I love about HippopotamUS!

Hippopotamus is Greek for "river horse." They spend about 16 hours submerged in water!

Like knowing how to have fun, even in the REINDEER.

In the winter, male reindeer shed their antlers.

Or winging a FLAMINGO dance.

Flamingos get their pink color from the brine shrimp they eat.

15

I especially love LION around and watching the sunset with you.

Lions are the only cats that live in groups called prides.

I can't wait to travel to new places and SEAL the world together.

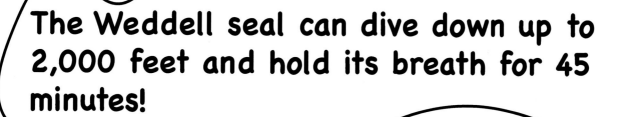

The Weddell seal can dive down up to 2,000 feet and hold its breath for 45 minutes!

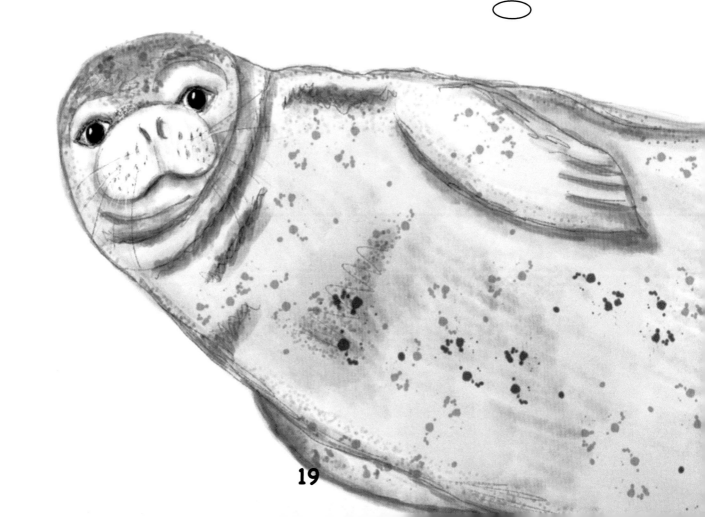

I GORILLA crazy when I'm with you because your love makes me go bananas.

There are only several hundred mountain gorillas remaining on earth— we need to protect them!

21

That being said, there's nothing like a lazy GIRAFFEternoon and getting to relOX with you.

Giraffes can grow to be about 19 feet tall and have tongues about 2 feet long!

OWL never get tired of hanging out with you.

I can spend

COWntless

hours with you.

There are 1.4 billion cows on farms through out the world.

But thanks for GIBBON me little reminders to catch some CHIMPANZzzzs.

Chimpanzee's mothers carry their babies on their back for 4 years or more.

The more KOALATY time we spend together, the more I realize you'll always have my back.

On a hot day, Koalas will hug trees to cool off.

I can't BEAR to BEE away from you.

Male brown bears can grow to be 10 feet tall and weigh over 1,200 pounds.

33

"You're my best pal,

and I DOGgone love you.

The Dog was the first domesticated animal—that's probably over 10,000 years of best friendship!

I sure RAM glad there's you because...

The ram has amazing vision which helps them move easily through rocky, mountain terrain.

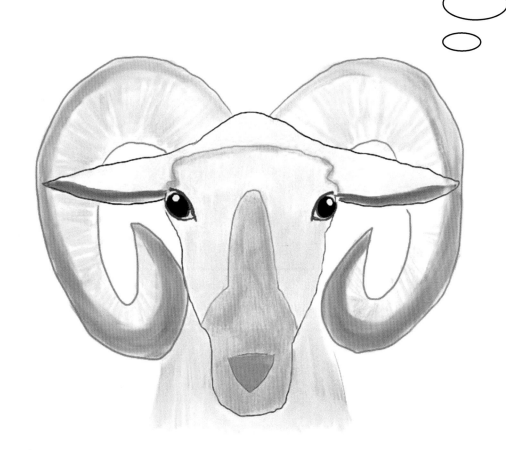

TOUCAN do more than one can.

The toucan's beak can be as sharp as a knife—don't mess around with this bird!

There's definitely no OTTER pair, like you and me.

Otters sleep while floating on their backs.

The End.

Made in the USA
San Bernardino, CA
13 February 2018